W9-CMG-869

THE WICKED TRICKS OF TYL UILENSPIEGEL

THE WICKED TRICKS OF TYL UILENSPIEGEL

by JAY WILLIAMS

illustrated by

FRISO HENSTRA

Four Winds Press New York

"Duke Pishposh of Pash," "Doctor Tyl," and "The Christmas Thief" have previously appeared in Cricket Magazine.

PUBLISHED BY FOUR WINDS PRESS
A DIVISION OF SCHOLASTIC MAGAZINES, INC., NEW YORK, N.Y.

PRINTED IN THE UNITED STATES OF AMERICA
LIBRARY OF CONGRESS CATALOG CARD NUMBER: 77–7884

1 2 3 4 5 82 81 80 79 78

LIBRARY OF CONGRESS CATALOGING IN PUBLICATION DATA
Williams, Jay.
The wicked tricks of Tyl Uilenspiegel.
Contents: Tyl on a tightrope. —Doctor Tyl. —Duke Pishposh of Pash. —The Christmas thief.
1. Eulenspiegel, Till—Legends. [1. Eulenspiegel, Till. 2. Folklore–Germany] I. Eulenspiegel. II. Henstra, Friso. III. Title.
PZ8.1W652Wi [398.2] [E] 77–7884
ISBN 0–590–07478–4

BY THE SAME AUTHOR

The Hero from Otherwhere

The Hawkstone

People of the Ax

Battle for the Atlantic

co-author of the Danny Dunn books

Everyone Knows What a Dragon Looks Like

The Burglar Next Door

The Reward Worth Having

The Time of the Kraken

CONTENTS

AUTHOR'S NOTE

Tyl Uilenspiegel was as famous in the Netherlands as Robin Hood was in England. Like Robin, Tyl was a jolly rogue, but where Robin traditionally stole from the rich and gave to the poor, Tyl stole from everyone and kept it for himself. His name means "Owl's Mirror," that is, the moon. During the long war for independence which the Low Countries fought against Spain in the sixteenth century, there were many popular tales in which Tyl was made the symbol of the cunning and boldness of the Netherlanders.

THE WICKED TRICKS OF TYL UILENSPIEGEL

TYL ON A TIGHTROPE

One fine morning, a large sign was posted up in the market square of the town of Edam:

NEVER BEFORE IN HISTORY SO DARING A FEAT!

The Famous Juggler **TYL UILENSPIEGEL** *will walk a 30 foot rope*

!!! BLINDFOLD !!!

The people began to gather, staring and pointing and chattering. When the square was almost filled, Tyl himself appeared, a tall, thin, sharp-nosed man with a wicked but merry face.

"Now, good people," he called, "step back and give me room."

He took off his hat and bowed. Holding out the hat, he began to move among the crowd.

"I cannot perform this difficult and dangerous stunt for nothing, you know," he said. "If I fall and break my neck, I must leave something for my poor old mother to live on."

Everyone put a little money into the hat until at last it was full. Tyl stuffed the coins in his purse. He picked up a coil of rope and stretched it out flat on the ground. Taking a red kerchief from around his neck, he tied it over his eyes. Then, quickly, he walked along the rope.

He pulled off the kerchief and made a low bow. "I thank you," said he, and started to leave.

Shouts arose: "Cheat! Robber! Give us back our money!"

A fat butcher caught Tyl by one arm and a skinny tailor seized him by the other. They dragged him away to the judge and everyone followed, yelling and shaking their fists.

"But, Your Worship, I've done nothing wrong," Tyl said, looking surprised. "I don't know what all the fuss is about. I said I would walk along a thirty-foot rope blindfolded, and that's just what I did. You can measure the rope if you don't believe me."

A Spanish soldier peered out. He looked around and saw nobody but Tyl, dripping wet. "What are you doing here?" he demanded.

"Let me in," said Tyl. "I'm a poor wandering juggler and acrobat. If you'll give me dinner, I'll give a show in return."

"Good," said the soldier. "It's very boring here. We could do with some entertainment."

He led Tyl into the courtyard, where the other soldiers crowded around to see who had come. Their captain appeared.

"What can you do?" he asked Tyl.

"I can walk a tightrope between two of those towers, high above the courtyard," said Tyl, boldly.

"I'd like to see that," said the captain, and he ordered some soldiers to stretch a rope across the towers from one window to another.

Now Tyl had never really walked a tightrope in his life, and he began to shiver with fright. However, he said to himself, "There must be a first time for everything," so up he went to the top of one of the towers and stepped out of the window on the rope.

At first, the rope swayed back and forth under his feet. He held out his arms and balanced himself. He was graceful and light on his feet and he soon got the knack of how to walk, one small step at a time, along the rope. When he came to the middle, he looked down. He gulped, and his legs shook so that he almost fell.

"Ooooh!" said all the soldiers, far below, and they moved hastily out of the way.

But Tyl caught his balance again and walked on until he came to the other tower. There he sat down on the windowsill and wiped his damp forehead.

"Very good," said the Spanish captain, while the troops laughed and applauded.

Tyl called down, "I will now do my most famous trick. It is called *High Boots*. I have performed it before the kings and queens of Europe, the Sultan of Turkey, and even the Emperor of China, and now for the very first time I will show it to the brave soldiers of Spain and their gallant commander. But—" he added, holding up a hand to stop their applause, "I need your help."

"What can we do?" said the captain. "None of us can walk a tightrope."

"You won't have to do anything like that," said Tyl. "For this trick, every man must take off one of his boots. I will collect them all, and while dancing on the rope I will make the boots fly through the air."

"Remarkable!" said the captain. "I can hardly believe it."

"You'll be surprised," Tyl said, with a grin.

He came down into the courtyard, while every soldier took

off one of his heavy boots. Tyl put them all into a bag. He went up to the top of the tower and carefully stepped out on the rope again.

He was more sure of himself this time. He walked out to the center of the rope, holding the bag. He lifted one foot—the rope jiggled. The watching soldiers held their breath.

He put that foot down and lifted the other. The rope joggled.

"So much for the dancing," said Tyl. "And now, I will make the boots fly through the air."

He turned the bag upside down and shook it. Out fell the boots, dozens and dozens of them. They showered on the heads of the soldiers and scattered all over the courtyard.

"End of the show!" called Tyl, merrily. "Find your own boots."

Some of the soldiers cursed, others laughed. They hopped about, snatching up boots and trying them on, then throwing them away and scrambling after others.

While this was going on, Tyl had been busy. As soon as he had dropped the boots, he had run along the rope and into the tower. He ran down the stairs and then along the wall until he came to another stair that led to the gates. No one was paying any attention to him. A great beam held the gates shut. Softly, Tyl pushed it to one side. Nearby, a thick rope came down to a windlass. This rope held up the drawbridge. Tyl took out a little knife he always carried and with one slash cut the rope. Down fell the bridge with a rattle and a crash.

The men of Edam were waiting. When the bridge dropped, they charged forward with yells and cheers. The soldiers had heard the noise of the bridge and were in confusion, not knowing what was happening, still trying to find their boots, stumbling and bumping into each other. The people ran across the bridge waving their swords and spears, and pushed against the gates which flew open, letting them into the courtyard. A few of the Spaniards tried to fight but were overpowered. The rest, finding themselves surrounded, threw down their weapons and surrendered.

"The city is ours!" shouted the butcher.

The tailor, who was carrying a sword almost as big as himself, clapped Tyl on the back. "I was wrong," he said. "You are as

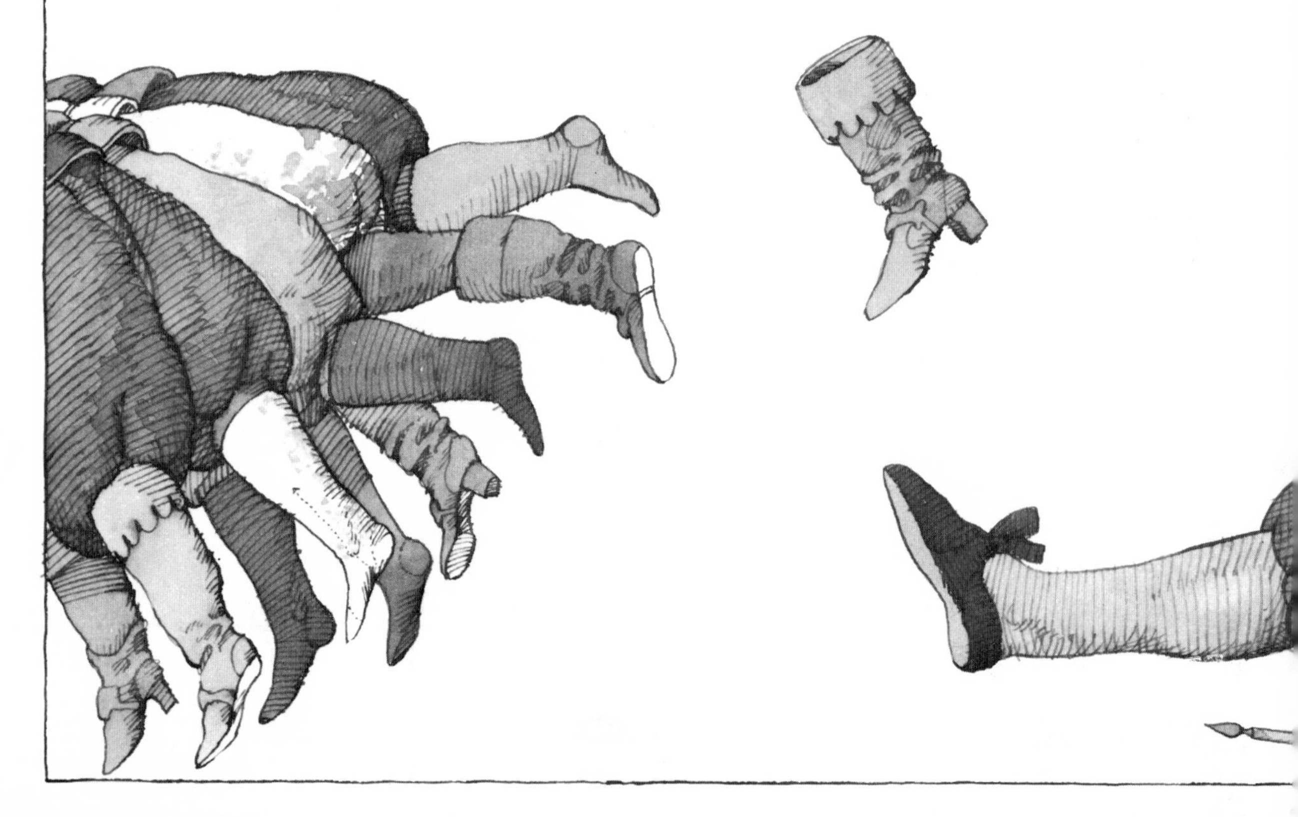

good a Hollander as anyone here. You kept your promise, and we'll keep ours. When we get back to Edam, you shall have your money."

"I'll make another promise," said Tyl. He looked up at the rope which stretched from tower to tower, high above their heads. "I promise I'll never walk another tightrope again."

DOCTOR TYL

The rain came drizzling down from the gray clouds, turning the dusty road to mud. It dripped from the sails of windmills and from the hat of Tyl Uilenspiegel as he trudged along, cold and wet and hungry.

He came, at last, to a little inn on the edge of a town. He went inside and shook the rain off his hat. A fire was burning on the hearth and he stood before it. His clothes began to steam as they dried. He had only one gulden in his purse and he tossed it to the innkeeper and asked for some bread and cheese, and a pot of beer.

"Now, Tyl," he said to himself, "you will have to use your wits, for you have nothing else left."

When he had had something to eat and drink, he felt better. He said to the innkeeper, "What is this town like? Are there many rich people in it?"

The innkeeper laughed bitterly. "Not any more," said he. "Not since the Spanish governor has come with all his troops. He has taken everyone's money and put it in his own treasury. He has taken the burgomaster's house for himself, and his officers live in the houses of the merchants. He has even moved all our sick people to a big barn, so that he can use the hospital for his soldiers."

"I see," said Tyl. "He sounds like just the sort of man I want to meet. Tell me, is there a doctor in the town?"

"There are two," the innkeeper replied. "There is the Spanish doctor in the hospital, but he only looks after the troops. And there is good old Doctor Ketel, who would give you the shirt off his back if you needed it."

"Show me where Doctor Ketel lives," said Tyl, "for there's

something I must get from him."

Soon afterward, Tyl knocked at the doctor's door. He had left his coat at the inn and wore only his shirt, and he was shivering and shaking. Old Doctor Ketel came to the door and looked at him sympathetically.

"Please, can you loan me an old coat? I am freezing," said Tyl, with chattering teeth.

"Of course, my poor man," said the doctor. He brought out a long black robe such as doctors wore, and gave it to Tyl. "You may keep it," he said.

Tyl put on the robe. Out of his pocket he took a pair of spectacles with plain glass in them, and perched them on his nose. They made him look very wise. Then he went to the hospital. He strode up to the doors with dignity and asked to see the doctor in charge. The sentry led him to a room in which sat a pale, nervous-looking man with a long gray beard that hung from his chin like moss.

"I am Doctor Almendras," he said, rising. "I see by your robe that you are also a doctor."

Tyl nodded. "I am no other than Doctor Grandiosus. No doubt you have heard of me."

"Of course," said the other. He was too timid to admit that he didn't know so important a man.

"And so," Tyl went on, "you know that I can cure anyone of anything. My specialty, as it happens, is military diseases. If you have any soldiers who are sick, I will absolutely guarantee to make them well."

"We have a hundred and ten soldiers in the hospital," said Doctor Almendras. "But I can't believe that you can cure them all."

"We shall see," said Tyl. "My fee is high, one gold piece for each man. But if I fail, you needn't pay me. What can be fairer than that?"

Now Tyl knew very well that the soldiers were tired of fighting and wanted to avoid work, so they either pretended to be sick or made the slightest little pain seem much worse than it was. He followed Doctor Almendras to the ward, a very long room in which were a hundred and ten beds with a soldier in every one of them.

"I must be left alone," he told Doctor Almendras. "My method is a secret."

Doctor Almendras bowed and left the ward. Then Tyl put a screen around the first man's bed so that no one could see him or hear him. He sat down beside the soldier, felt his pulse, and looked at his tongue.

Then he said, softly, "My friend, I am Doctor Grandiosus, and I have a perfect cure for every disease. I like your looks, and so I'm going to tell you a secret. My famous medicine is made by

taking a man and pounding him to a paste and then mixing him with fish-fur and snake's ears."

"A man?" said the soldier, beginning to tremble. "What man?"

"I will choose the sickest patient in the hospital," said Tyl.

He left that soldier, and put the screen around the next bed. He told the same thing to the second soldier, and then to the third, and so on until he had told it to all one hundred and ten.

Then he called Doctor Almendras, and said, "Everything is ready. I have given each man my special treatment, and now they're cured."

"What?" cried Doctor Almendras. "So quickly? It's not possible."

"You shall see," said Tyl. And turning round, he said in a loud voice, "All those who are well may leave the hospital. The sick men may stay."

At once, every single man jumped out of bed. None of them wanted to be left behind to be pounded to a paste and mixed with fish-fur and snake's ears, and they almost fell over each other in their hurry to get as far away as possible.

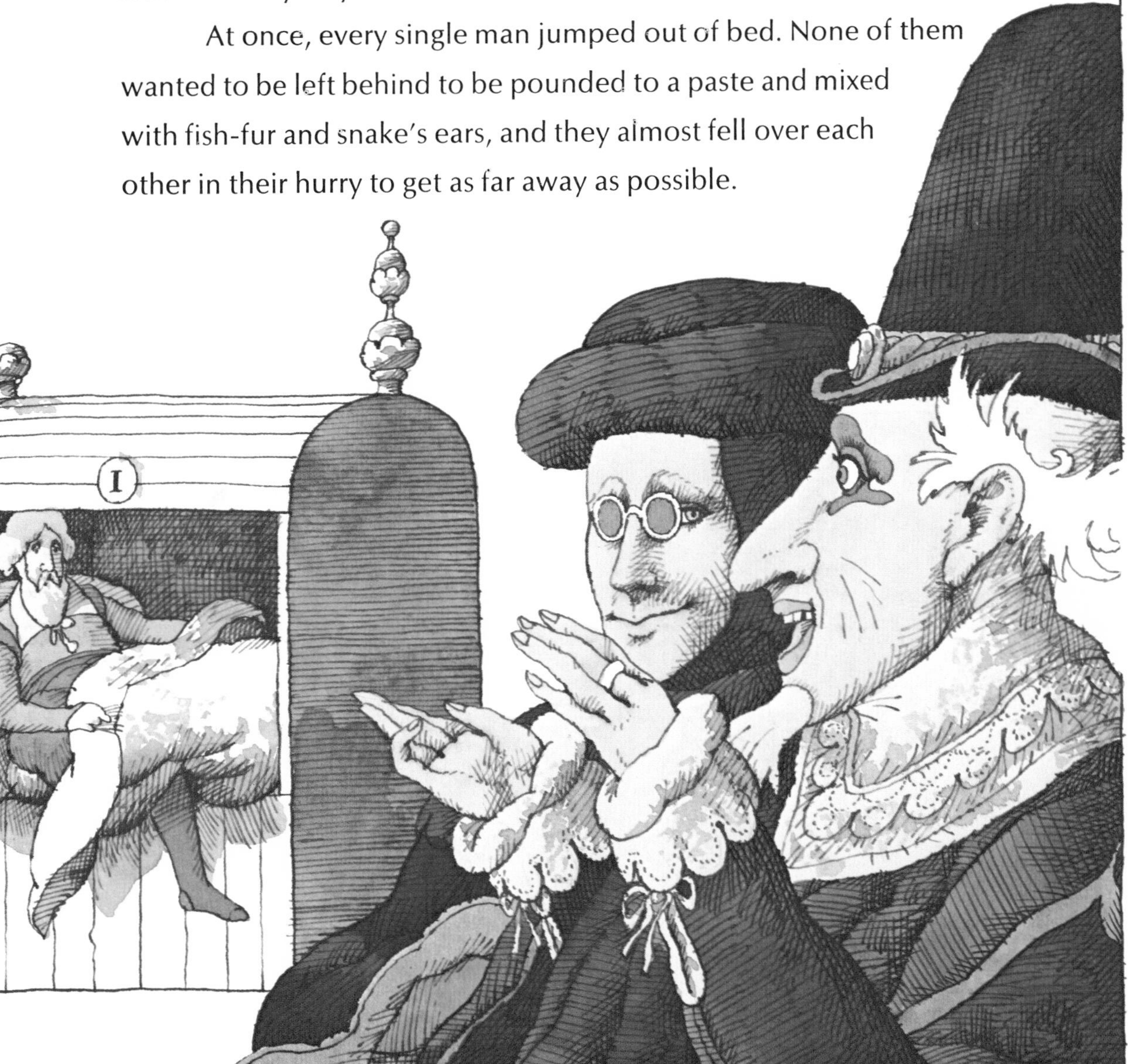

"Marvelous!" said Doctor Almendras, staring at the empty

beds. "You must come with me to the governor. He is always complaining that he doesn't feel well, and I can't do anything for him. You are just the man he needs."

"I think so, too," said Tyl. "But first, you owe me a hundred and ten gold pieces."

The doctor gave him the money. Then he led the way from the hospital to the fine, big house which had once belonged to the burgomaster but was now the governor's. Up the stairs they went, past the guards at the outer door, and the guards at the inner door, and the guards in the hall, and the guards on the staircase, and at last they came to the governor's office.

The governor was a portly man whose belly was so big that he could not button his gold-embroidered coat. He wore a white ruff on which his round head rested like a plum pudding on a plate. In front of him was half a roast goose, a whole joint of beef, and a pitcher of wine.

"What do you want?" he growled. "I'm busy."

Doctor Almendras said, "I have brought a wonderful new doctor, Doctor Grandiosus, who has cured all the patients in my hospital."

The governor jumped up, puffing, and seized Tyl by the hand.

"My dear sir," he said, "I am delighted to see you. I have many illnesses and no one can do anything to help me."

"I'll see what I can do," said Tyl.

The governor waved to Doctor Almendras, who bowed and departed. Tyl frowned through his spectacles, and said, "Tell me what ails you."

"Well, in the first place," said the governor, "whenever I eat too much I feel very full. And when I drink too much wine, I get terrible headaches. I can't sleep more than nine hours a night, and then I'm awake all day. Smoke from a chimney makes me sneeze, and roast peacock gives me a rash."

Tyl nodded, gravely. "It's a lucky thing for you I'm here," he said. "Those are the symptoms of the dread piggish-pox."

"But doctor," whined the governor, "there's another problem. I can't stand all those nasty medicines. They taste so awful, I'd rather be sick."

"My medicine will be different," promised Tyl. "Put on your night-shirt and get into bed, while I prepare it for you."

He went to the kitchen and said to the head cook, "Bring me all the sugar you have."

The cook gave him a big bag full. He put it into a pot over the fire, and boiled it until it had become a thick, gummy mass of taffy. He let it cool. He put some butter on his hands to keep them from sticking to it, and made it into a ball. He took it to the governor's bedroom.

The governor was in bed, as he had been told. "Open your mouth," Tyl commanded.

The governor did so. At once, Tyl crammed the whole ball of taffy into it.

"Uh-gug!" roared the governor. His teeth were stuck tightly together. He tried to pull the taffy out, but his fingers stuck to it, as well. He fell out of bed, still roaring.

"I hope that's sweet enough for you," said Tyl. "And now, while you are being cured of your piggishness, I will just pay myself for my trouble."

He opened the governor's iron strong box, and helped himself to a bag of gold. Meanwhile, the governor was jumping from one foot to the other, trying to pry his jaws apart.

"Good-bye," said Tyl. "You won't be able to eat so much for a while, and that will make you feel better."

He let himself out of the bedroom. The guards at the door stood at attention.

Tyl said, "Your master, the governor, has a high fever which is making him delirious. Fetch some buckets of cold water, at once!"

The guards dropped their halberds and ran off. In a few moments, they returned, each carrying two buckets.

"Good," said Tyl. "Go inside and pour the water over him slowly, and don't stop until I tell you to."

He held the bedroom door open for them, and closed it behind them. Inside, he could hear the splashing of water and the bawling of the governor.

"I hope no one will ever say I don't do good deeds," chuckled Tyl, as he hurried away. "For I have cured a hundred and eleven people in one morning, which is more than any other doctor can boast of."

DUKE PISHPOSH OF PASH

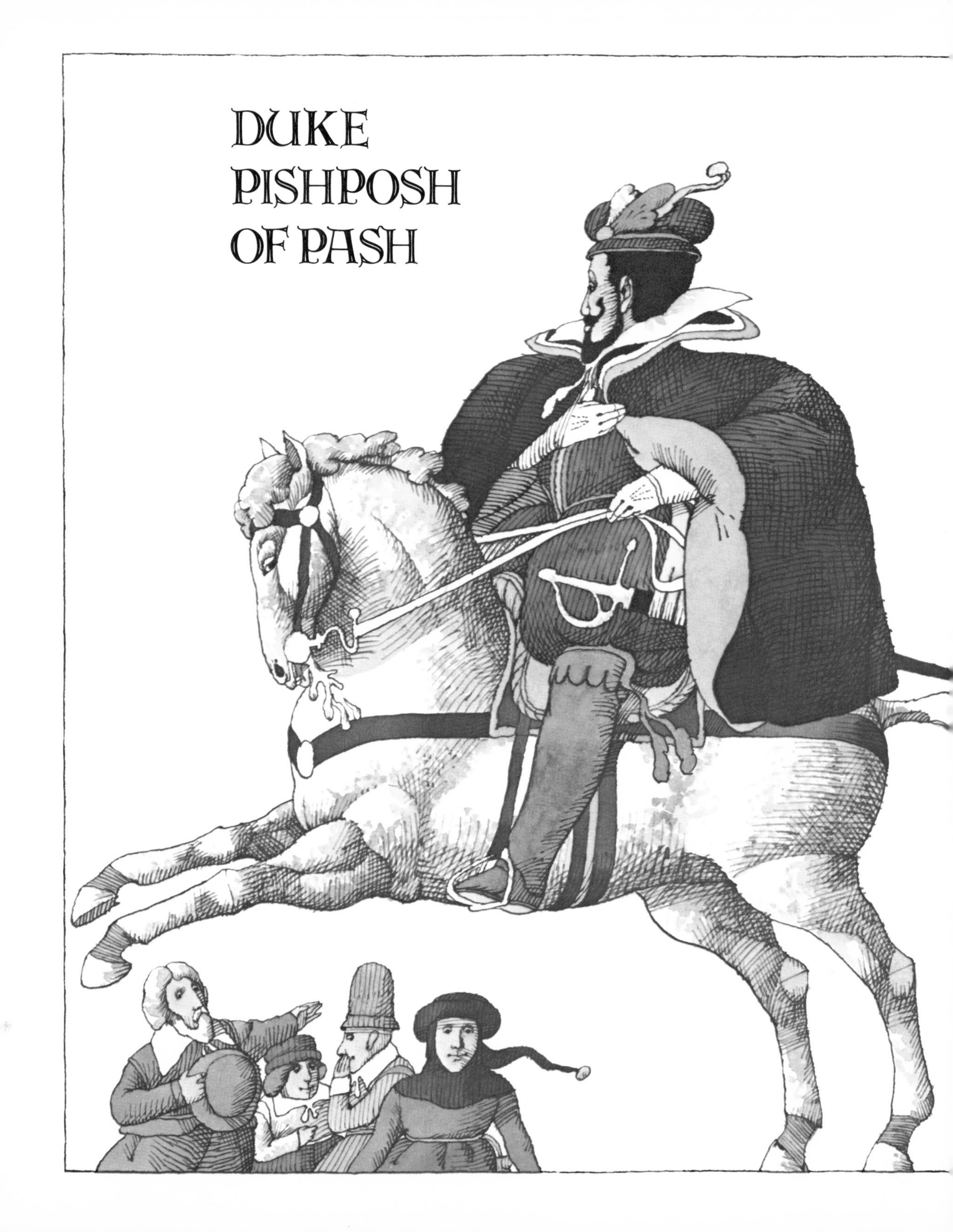

On a day in early spring, Prince William of Orange rode into the city of Delft. He was the leader of the armies of the Netherlands, and he was on his way to Amsterdam to meet with his captains. As he went through the square on his way to the burgomaster's house, he heard a commotion: a small crowd surrounded a man in a bright red jacket, and some were arguing at the tops of their voices, and some were laughing.

The prince rode to the spot and commanded them to be silent. They recognized him and fell back quietly.

"What is happening here?" he asked.

One man stepped forward. "Your Highness," said he, "I am a cheese merchant. This fellow in the red coat told me he had a perfect way of getting rid of mice. He said it was guaranteed to work every time, and so I bought it for a hundred florins. This is what he gave me. It's a swindle!"

He held out a hammer and a block of wood. "He told me to put each mouse on the block of wood and hit it with the hammer," he finished.

Prince William could not help laughing. "He was right, it will work every time. But you are right, too—it was a swindle." He looked at the man in the red jacket. "What is your name?" he said.

"Tyl Uilenspiegel, Your Highness," said Tyl, with a low bow.

"I have heard of you," said the prince, frowning. "Return this man's money, and come with me."

Tyl did not dare to disobey, and he followed the prince to the burgomaster's house.

There, Prince William said, sternly, "You are a rogue and a trickster. Can you give me any reason why I should not send you to prison?"

"It's not my fault, Your Highness," said Tyl. "It's just that everyone I meet is so foolish. All I have to do is ask, and they give me money. Why, I'll wager I can get the richest man in Delft to give me anything I want."

"I can't believe it," said the prince. "If you can do such a thing, I'll set you free."

"Very well," Tyl said. "All I need is five gold pieces to start with."

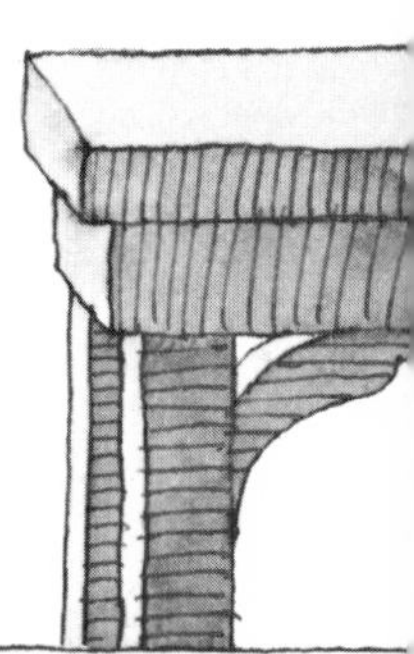

The prince gave them to him, and said, "I must stay in Delft for two days. That is all the time you have."

"It's enough," said Tyl.

The richest man in Delft was named Lucas Koop. He was suspicious and bad-tempered, and very stingy. He lived in a fine big house and spent much of his time counting his money, and the rest of his time dreaming of ways of getting more. Next door to his big house was a little house belonging to a poor shoemaker, Jan Brouwer. Jan was hardworking, kind, warmhearted, and the biggest gossip in town.

That night, a ragged beggar with a patch over one eye knocked at the shoemaker's door. "I have traveled many miles and I have no money," he said. "Please let me warm myself at your fire for a little while."

"Come in, come in," said the shoemaker. "You must be hungry too, and you're just in time for supper. We haven't much, but what there is you're welcome to share."

In came Tyl—for, of course, it was he. The shoemaker's wife greeted him, and the shoemaker's two children stared at him in curiosity. He warmed himself before the fire and told them stories of his travels, and they listened in wonder for they had never been away from Delft. Then they all sat down to a simple meal of bread and sausages and beer, and if there wasn't much to eat, there was plenty of friendliness to season it.

After dinner, Tyl said, "I thank you, good people. Now I must be on my way again."

"Nonsense!" said Jan Brouwer. "The night is cold and dark, and I wouldn't think of turning you out into it. We haven't any

spare beds, but you are welcome to some straw before the fire, and a blanket."

He filled a bag with straw and gave Tyl a blanket. Tyl rolled up on the hearth and slept soundly, for he had slept in many worse places.

In the morning, they had bread and milk for breakfast, and then Tyl stood up, looking suddenly much taller and more dignified.

"I have something to tell you," he said, to the shoemaker. "I am no beggar, but Duke Pishposh of Pash. Every spring, I travel about in disguise looking for people who are kind and generous, and when I find them, I reward them for each thing they give me. You have given me five things—a roof over my head, a good dinner, a fire, a bed, and breakfast. Here are five gold pieces."

He put the money into the shoemaker's hand. The poor man stared, and his wife and children stared, too, for they had never before seen so much gold all at once.

Then Tyl left them, and all that day the shoemaker could not keep from telling everyone he met about his good fortune. So it wasn't long before the news reached his rich neighbor next door.

That night, Tyl, still dressed in beggar's rags and with a patch over one eye, knocked at the door of Lucas Koop's house. A servant appeared.

"The night is cold and my way is hard," said Tyl. "Please may I come in and warm myself?"

The servant bowed. "My master has given orders that any ragged beggar—and especially one with a patch over his eye—should be admitted. Come in, and I will take you to him."

Tyl grinned to himself, and followed the servant into a paneled room full of splendid furniture and hung with paintings. In a big tiled stove, a good fire was throwing out plenty of heat. Lucas Koop was standing before the stove and when he saw Tyl he came forward to greet him, trying to smile although he had no practice at it.

"Welcome!" he croaked. "Glad to see you. I am always kind to beggars, and anyone will tell you that I am the most generous man in the world. I'm sure you must be hungry—"

"That's right," said Tyl.

"Then come this way." And Koop led him into a dining room where, at a long table, a feast was spread.

"What handsome silver dishes these are," said Tyl.

"Do you like them? Please take one as a gift," Koop said.

After he had eaten as much as he could hold, Tyl said, "Now I must be on my way again."

"No, no," said Koop. "You are my guest. I have a bedroom specially prepared for you."

He showed Tyl a room in which there was a big four-poster bed, spread with linen sheets and heaped with feather quilts. On a table beside the bed were a bowl of fruit, a pitcher of wine, and a silver goblet.

"What a beautiful goblet," said Tyl.

"Do you like it? Please take it as a gift," said Koop. "Anything in the house is yours. Help yourself."

And in his head, he added up the number of gold pieces he would get the next morning from Duke Pishposh of Pash.

But the next morning, his guest was gone. So were the silver dish, the silver goblet, a gold tobacco box, a fine candlestick, and a great many other expensive things. On the table was a note which said, "Come to the burgomaster's house for your reward. Duke Pishposh of Pash."

Full of joy, Lucas Koop scurried to the burgomaster's house. There he found Prince William of Orange having breakfast with

the beggar, who no longer had a patch over his eye, and wore a red jacket instead of rags.

"Here is the man I was telling you about," said Tyl to the prince, as Lucas Koop came in. "He is the rich man who gave me the things in this sack."

He picked up a bag in which were the silver dish, the silver goblet, the tobacco box, the candlestick, and all the rest.

"Is that true?" the prince asked.

"Yes, Your Highness," answered Koop.

"There you are," said Tyl. "And what's more, I didn't even have to ask him for anything. He gave me a splendid dinner and a soft bed, and told me to help myself to anything in the house. Isn't that so?"

THE CHRISTMAS THIEF

A light frosting of snow lay over the little town of Sterkdam. It was the day before Christmas, and everyone was feeling sad.

Circling the town was a Spanish army, hundreds of fierce soldiers well armed with muskets, pikes, and swords. Worse still, they had twelve great cannons which shot iron balls over the walls of the town, battering the houses and knocking down the chimneys. But the brave people of Sterkdam refused to surrender.

They kept their gates closed so the Spaniards could not enter. At the same time, the Spaniards would let no one leave. Soon, food began to run short and by now there was nothing left to eat. Everyone was hungry, from the burgomaster and the rich merchants, to the old man who made baskets. Even in the town prison, the one single prisoner was hungry.

It was Tyl. He had come to Sterkdam before the siege began, and now he could not leave. He had no money, and so he had stolen a pair of wooden shoes in broad daylight, right under the nose of the Chief Watchman so that he would be arrested and put in prison. There, he thought he would have shelter in a warm place and something to eat, but now they could not give him so much as a crust of bread.

He stood at the barred window looking at the clear blue sky and sighing. A boy came into sight in the street below, hugging his stomach and weeping.

"What's the matter with you?" Tyl asked, looking down.

"I'm hungry," said the boy. "And tomorrow is Christmas. There will be no presents and no Christmas dinner. Not even Saint Nicholas will be able to get into this town with the Spaniards all around it."

Tyl stared at the boy, and thought about the children of the town. "Maybe I can do something about it," he said. "But you must help me. Get me a pail of blue paint and a brush, and come back here as quickly as you can."

Away sped the boy. Soon he returned with the paint and brush. Around his waist Tyl carried a long, thin cord. He uncoiled it and lowered it through the bars.

"Put the brush in the pail and tie the handle of the pail to the cord," he said.

When the boy had done so, Tyl pulled up the pail. He painted the bars of his window blue, the same color as the sky. Then he stood in a corner behind the door of the cell and shouted, as loudly as he could, "Good-bye! I'm going!"

The guard heard him and came running. He unlocked the door and opened it. When he looked in, he saw a window without bars—for the blue bars did not show against the blue sky. "The prisoner has escaped!" he cried, and rushed off for help, leaving the cell door open. Tyl strolled quietly out of the prison and into the street. He took with him the sheet from the bed.

There were townspeople on the walls of the city, all armed in case the Spaniards attacked. There were more people guarding the great main gate. And there was one man with a musket guarding the little iron door that opened on the river. He was hungry and cold and drowsy.

Tyl walked up to him, and said, boldly, "What are you doing?"

The man straightened. "My orders are not to let anyone in through this gate," he replied.

"Good," said Tyl. "Then open it, for I am already in, and I am going out."

The man unbolted the gate. "The Spaniards will kill you," he warned.

"They will if they see me," said Tyl, "but I won't let them

see me."

He put the bed sheet over his head. Against the white snow, he was invisible. As softly as a flake of snow, he walked to the frozen river and crossed it. He was going to the one place where there was plenty of food—the Spanish camp.

The Spaniards were preparing for their Christmas Eve feast. At blazing bonfires they roasted meat, and cooked rich stews in iron pots. Tyl crept up to the nearest tent and with his little knife cut a slit in the canvas. He peeped in; there was no one inside. He stepped through the slit. When he came out of the front of the tent, he was wearing a Spanish helmet and breastplate, and carrying a big cloak over one arm.

He walked boldly to one of the fires and helped himself to a piece of roast meat. One of the soldiers said, "Where are you going with that?"

"It's for the general," said Tyl, putting the meat into the cloak.

He went to the other fire and took a roast chicken. "For the general," he said.

Soon the cloak was full of food. He found a quiet corner

and hid the food, and off he went again with the empty cloak.

Here and there he went, as lightly as a feather, as quietly as a puff of smoke. He slipped into tents and took sweetmeats and little cakes, strings of sausages, loaves of bread, hard round cheeses. At the fires, he collected roast geese, legs of lamb, slices of beef. He hid them all away in different places. Whenever anyone stopped him, he said, "For the general," and they saluted and let him go.

From the general's tent, he quietly took an enormous Christmas pudding. As he was leaving the tent with the pudding wrapped in his cloak, a soldier said, "What have you got there?"

"A present from the general to the captain," said Tyl, and went on his way.

As darkness fell, the Spaniards began to eat their dinners. The cannons were pointing at the town walls, but nobody was near them for on Christmas Eve they saw no reason to fire them off. However, they were loaded and ready.

Tyl went up to the first cannon. He took out the cannonball and in its place crammed the barrel with food. He did the same to the next, and the next, until all twelve cannons were filled with food instead of cannonballs. Then he went looking for the Chief of Artillery.

The Chief of Artillery had finished his dinner and was drinking a cup of wine beside a fire.

"Sir," said Tyl, saluting him, "I bring a message from the general. Tonight, you are to fire all your cannons once at the city, to show them they can have no rest."

"But how can we see where to aim in the darkness?" asked the Chief of Artillery.

"That's my job," said Tyl. "I will sneak into the town and light a torch on the top of the church tower. You can aim at the light, and you must fire all the cannons together."

"You are a brave man," said the Captain of Artillery.

"Yes, I know," said Tyl, modestly. "Be ready for my signal."

He took off the helmet and armor. Then, softly, in the dark,

like the shadow of a soft-winged owl, he went back to the town.

Near the walls stood a tall windmill, its sails slowly turning in the night breeze. Tyl jumped up and caught the lowest sail. Up he went with it, higher and higher, until he was level with the top of the city wall. He leaped with all his might and fell sprawling on the hard stone.

No one saw him. The town was quiet. The people had gone to bed early with their hunger, and only one or two guards were still at the gates, half asleep.

Tyl made his way to the town square. He began to pound on the doors of houses, shouting, "Wake up! Wake up! Come out, come out!"

Doors and windows flew open. People looked out with torches and lanterns, asking, "What is it? What's happening?" They flocked into the street with their muskets and swords, thinking the Spanish army was attacking.

Tyl snatched a torch from someone and ran up the steps of the church. He stood before the doors where everyone could see him. "Listen!" he cried. "Saint Nicholas is coming."

The burgomaster was there in his nightcap. "Seize him!" he exclaimed. "It's the thief, Tyl Uilenspiegel. Arrest him!"

"Wait—" Tyl began.

But several men were advancing on him with their swords ready. Tyl turned and ran into the church. He ran to the door that led into the tower, with the men behind him. He slammed the door in their faces and bolted it.

Up the stairs he raced, until he came to the top of the tower where the great bells hung. He leaned out, holding his torch. The townspeople stared up at him with their mouths open. Tyl began waving the torch.

"Shoot him," commanded the burgomaster. "He is signaling to the enemy."

Muskets were raised. Men took aim. But before they could fire a shot—BOOM! came the crash of the Spanish cannons.

Swish! Out of the sky fell roast geese, roast chickens, roast beef, and loaves of bread. Nuts and candies pattered down like hail, and the children screamed with excitement as they scrambled for them. Cheeses bounced off the rooftops. A roast chicken fell into a woman's arms. A string of sausages wrapped itself around

a man's neck. The general's plum pudding hit the burgomaster

on the head and knocked him flat.

"Merry Christmas!" laughed Tyl, leaning from the tower.

Everyone cheered, and hurried to pick up the good things. Nobody slept in Sterkdam that night. A bonfire was lighted in the square, and everyone feasted.

At daybreak, as the bells rang out for Christmas, a great army of Netherlanders under Prince William came marching across the plain. The Spaniards were surprised and outnumbered, and although they fought bravely, they were forced to retreat, leaving

their tents, their cook-pots, and even their cannons behind. The gates of the town were opened at last, and the people welcomed their friends with joy.

The burgomaster hung a golden chain around Tyl's neck. On it was a medal of gold, on which were the words:

To the thief, Tyl Uilenspiegel,
who stole Christmas for the people of Sterkdam.